TOUCH THE EARTH

JULIAN LENNON

with Bart Davis illustrated by Smiljana Coh

Sky Pony Press,
New York, NY

To Mum, who gave me the vision to fly without wings.

We all live on planet Earth. Gently touch the Earth.
Now touch where you live.

Our planet needs your help.
Would you like to go on a helping adventure?

Shake the book to make it change into
the magic White Feather Flier.

The White Feather Flier will take you

on a journey to help the Earth.

Just press the FLY button and tilt the book up.

To guide the
White Feather Flier,
you need directions.

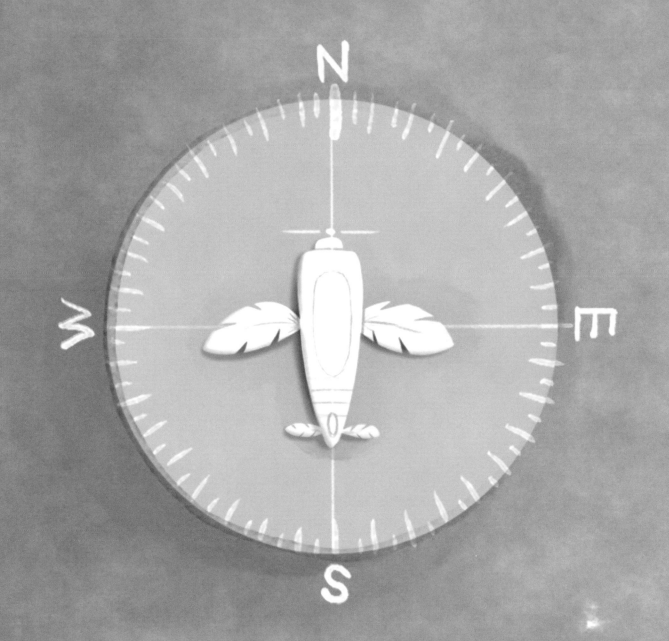

Point to all four directions on the compass and say their names: North, South, East, and West.

NORTH

WEST

EAST

SOUTH

Directions help us travel safely.

Tilt the book south and push
the LAND button to set it down.

Water is the most important resource on Earth.
But some places don't have enough
clean water for the people who live there.
Push the WATER button and make the water flow.

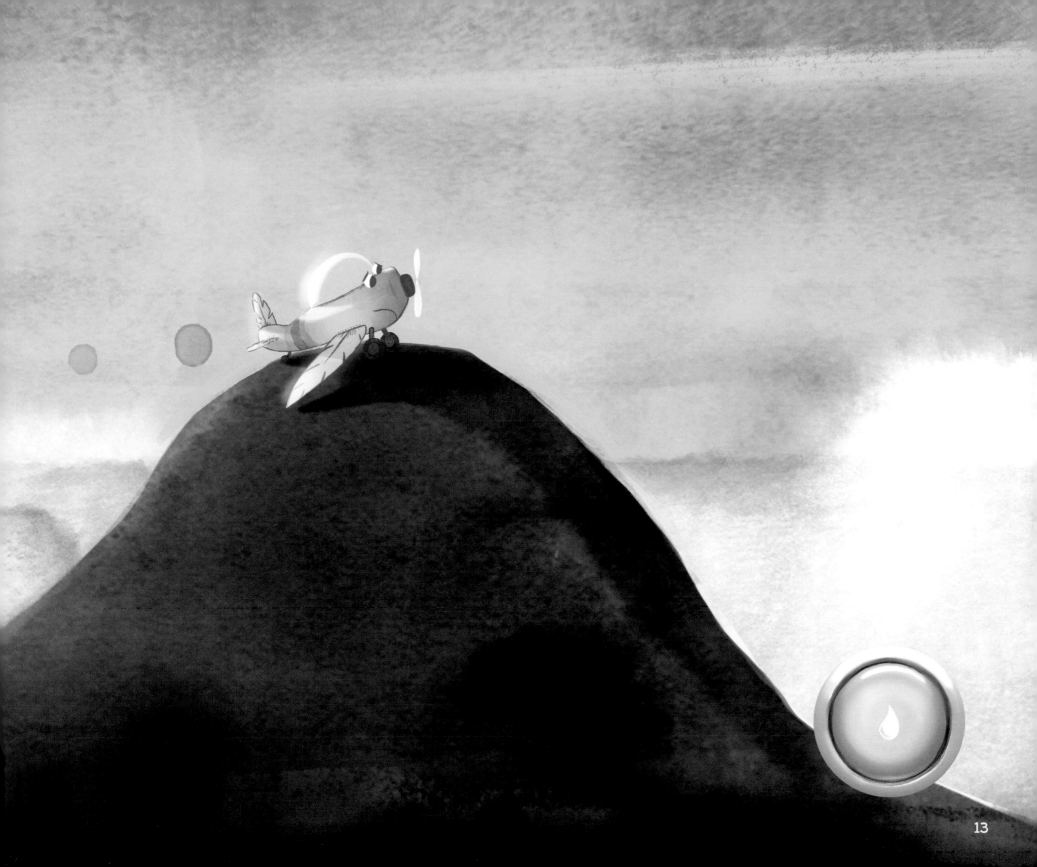

You did great! Now, there's enough water for people to drink!

Let's help our planet even more.
Push the FLY button and
tilt the book north.

The oceans touch every life on Earth.
Tilt the book south, and press
the DIVE button to take a trip under the sea.

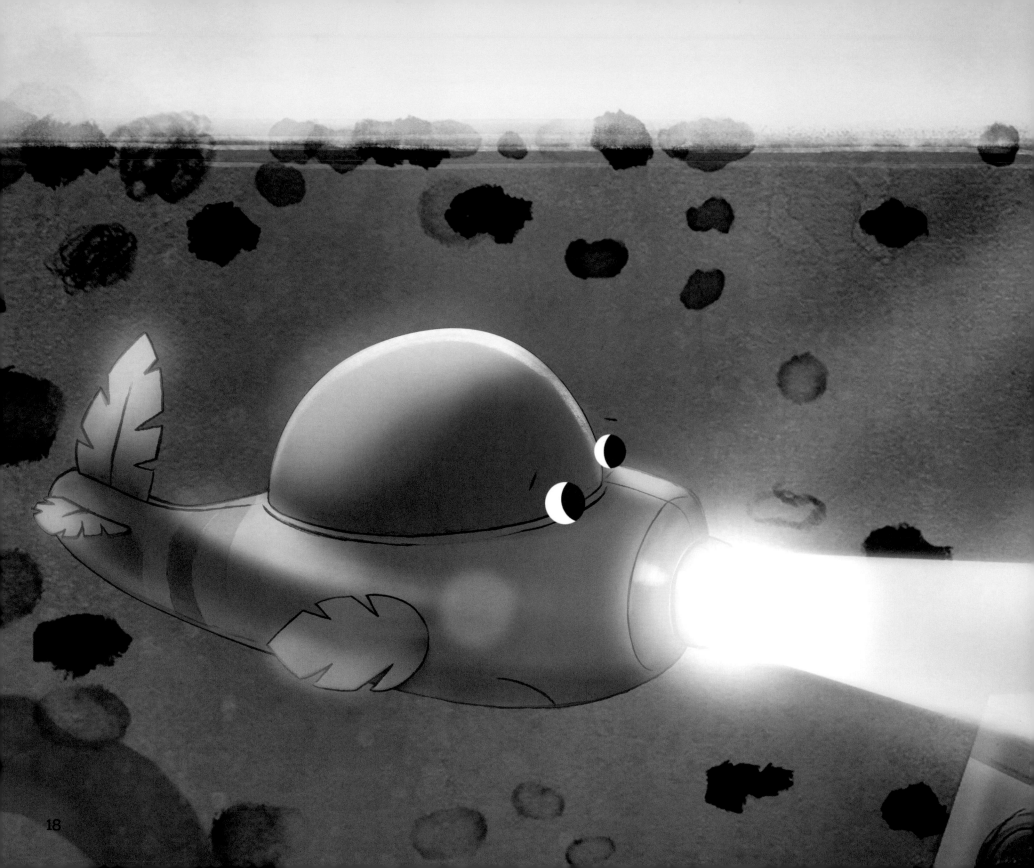

Fish are beautiful and important for so many people. We have to keep the water clean to protect the fish. Touch all the plastic bottles and things that shouldn't be in the water, and then push the FISH button to bring the fish back.

You've tipped the scales for sea creatures great and small. Would you like the adventure to continue?

Push the FLY button and
tilt the book east this time.

The desert is a place where there
is almost no water at all. Let's go and see.
Can you make a plan to land?
That's right, you know how!

Sometimes, we can bring water
to where the land is too dry,
like the desert.
It's called irrigation.
Push the WATER button
to help irrigate the desert.

You made the desert bloom like a garden. Now, it can grow food for people and animals.

Are you ready to see more?
Help the White Feather Flier
take off into the sky.

Rain is another kind of water
that we all need. It keeps the oceans
filled and the rivers flowing.

But not all water is okay to drink.
Point the book south to swoop down
low for a closer look.

In some places, wells have water that isn't safe
to drink. Did you know there are machines to help
make that water pure and safe again?
Turn the book west, and then push the
PARACHUTE button to deliver a machine.

See how it works? We call this filtration.
Push the WATER button

and follow the water as it changes from yucky to clean.

It's time to head back home.

You've touched the Earth in so many ways.

Bye for now. We'll be back soon!

TOUCH THE EARTH

Touch the Earth and make it better.
All of us can work together.
Shining stars from up above,
Take care of all the things we love.

Gently let the water flow
To help the planet live and grow.
Love the Earth, the moon and sun.
All the children can be one.

Touch the Earth, the sky above.
Hold the hands of those you love.
Dream a dream for me and you
Of love and friendship through and through.

To change the world for better days
We've got to learn to change our ways.
White Feather Flier can show us how
As we begin right here, right now . . .

Deepest oceans. Rivers flow.
So much to learn, to share and know.
North to south and east to west
We are part of all the rest.
Love the Earth, the moon and sun.
Hope all of us can be as one.
Rainbow colours, Spring and Fall.
Touch the Earth for one and all.

Julian Lennon

A Personal Message from Julian Lennon

"My dad once said to me that should he pass away, if there was some way of letting me know he was going to be okay—that we were all going to be okay—the message would come to me in the form of a White Feather. Then something remarkable happened to me. Whilst on tour in Australia, I was presented with a White Feather by an Aboriginal tribal elder of the Mirning people seeking help for her tribe. It definitely took my breath away.

Having the White Feather bestowed upon me, I knew this endeavor was to be part of my destiny from then on. It led me to create The White Feather Foundation to give a voice and support to those who cannot be heard. One thing for sure is that the White Feather has always represented peace to me and the message that it brings.

I believe that if we teach the children of the world to love and understand the planet, they will naturally want to take care of it. So follow the White Feather Flier and together we can touch the Earth and make it better . . . for everyone."

— Julian Lennon

To learn more about us, please visit
The White Feather Foundation at:

whitefeatherfoundation.com

THE
WHITE FEATHER
FOUNDATION